WHO CAN'T FOLLOW AN ANT?

Written by *Michael J. Pellowski*
Illustrated by *Susan Swan*

Troll Associates

Library of Congress Cataloging in Publication Data

Pellowski, Michael.
  Who can't follow an ant?

  Summary: Seven animal friends think they are going
to have an easy game when they start playing follow
the leader with an ant.
  [1. Play—Fiction. 2. Animals—Fiction. 3. Ants—
Fiction. 4. Stories in rhyme] I. Swan, Susan
Elizabeth, ill. II. Title.
PZ8.3.P35Wh   1986   [E]   85-14009
ISBN 0-8167-0592-5 (lib. bdg.)
ISBN 0-8167-0593-3 (pbk.)

WHO CAN'T FOLLOW AN ANT?

Turtle went to see his friends,
one warm and sunny day.
"This will be lots of fun,"
    he said.
"What shall we play today?"

Turtle's friends were there.
He saw Squirrel, Mole, and Hare.
Who else did he see?
Frog, Mouse, and Bear!

"What shall we do?" said Turtle.
"I know," said Mole.
"Let's have fun!
We'll dig a giant hole."

"Oh no!" said Hare.
"That's not fun.
Come on, my friends.
Let's all run!"

"Oh no," said Squirrel.
"Let's climb a tree.
Climbing trees is lots of fun.
Try it and you'll see."

"What can we play?" asked
    Frog.
The friends could not agree.
They wanted something fun
    for all.
What could that something be?
"You don't want to climb,"
    said Turtle.
"You don't want to dig or run.
So let's play a very special game.
A game that will be fun!"

"Good!" cried Mouse.
Frog yelled, "Hooray!
Let's get going right away."
"What game will we play?"
    asked Bear.
"What game will it be?"
"I don't know any games,"
    said Turtle.
His friends said, "Neither do we."
"Hey, want to play a game?"
    said someone.
"A good game that I know?
It's follow-the-leader.
Where I lead, you'll go."

"Who said that?" asked Turtle.
He looked up and down.
"Who knows a game?"
He looked all around.

"Hey, I know a game," said
　　someone once again.
"Look down here on the ground.
My game is follow-the-leader.
I will lead you all around."

15

They looked in the grass.
And what did they see?
There was an ant,
as small as could be.

"An ant!" said the bear.
"He won't do at all.
How can *he* lead a game?
He's very, very small!"

"Follow me," said the ant.
"My game is fun!
I am good at my game,
and I'll win when it's done."

"Lead on," said the friends.
"We will follow you, Ant.
You won't win this game.
Who can't follow an ant?"

Away went the ant.
Away he went fast.
He went over stones.
He went through the grass.

"What a game," said the friends.
"This is easy to do.
You can't win, Little Ant.
We can all follow you."

"Follow me," said the ant.
He went on and on.
He marched into some stickers.
And then he was gone.

Turtle went into the stickers.
So did Squirrel, Mole, and
    Hare.
Frog and Mouse went in, too.
But what about the bear?

Bear cried, "Ouch! That's not fair!
I can't follow an ant in there!"

"We can follow," said the rest.
"We still want to play.
We will follow and we'll win.
We'll follow you all day."

Now Ant crawled into a log,
deep into a hole.
Everybody liked it there,
especially the mole.
In went Squirrel, Mouse, and
        Hare.
They crawled inside the little hole
and came out over there.
In went the frog,
with one big jump.
But on his head he got a lump!
Jump! Bump! Jump! Thump!
        Jump! Lump!

"Ouch!" cried Frog.
"I can't go through.
You win, Little Ant.
I can't follow you."

Frog was now out.
And Bear was out, too.
The others were still following.
What would that ant do?

Mud can't stop an ant.
Ants are very small.
They don't get stuck in mud.
Over it they crawl.

Turtle and Mole crawled
through the mud.
They had very good luck.
Squirrel and Mouse crawled
through, too.
But the hare got stuck!

"I am stuck!" yelled Hare.
"I can't run or jump or crawl.
I can't follow an ant.
But good luck to you all!"

The ant looked back.
He said, "Follow me.
This game is not over."
Then he went up a tree.

Up the tree climbed the ant.
He climbed toward the sun.
Then down went the ant.
He still was not done.

Up climbed the squirrel.
The mouse climbed up, too.
But the mole and turtle could
    not climb.
Now what would they do?
"What a game!" cried Turtle.
"It's not easy to do."
"You win, Ant," said Mole.
"We can't follow you."

Mouse and Squirrel didn't stop.
They followed very fast.
The ant kept on going.
He hurried through the grass.

Squirrel asked, "Where is he
    going?"
"I do not know," said Mouse.
"Where am I going?" called
    the ant.
"I'm going in a house."

The squirrel stopped and looked.
A man's house he did see.
"I won't go there," the squirrel
    said.
"That's no place for me!"

"What a game," said the ant.
"It's a game that is fun.
I am good at my game.
And I'll win when it's done!"

The ant marched straight into
   the house.
The mouse went right in, too.
But in the house, there was a man.
What could that mouse do?

The man looked at the mouse.
The mouse looked at the man.
The man yelled, "Out of my
     house, Mouse!"
And out the mouse ran.
"You win," cried the mouse.
"I want to follow, but can't.
You went into a house.
In there, I can't follow an ant!"

Through the house went the ant.
He cried, "Hooray! Hooray!"
"Is the game over?" someone
     said.
"I still want to play."
"What?" cried the ant.
He looked up and down.
"Who wants to play?"

"I am here," someone said.
"I played your game, too.
You didn't see me.
But I followed you."
Ant said, "You're the winner.
The winner is you!
But what do you look like?
Why, you're an ant, too!"

I am here.
I played your game, too.
You didn't see me.
But I followed you.